DREAM HOP

By Julia Durango · Illustrated by Jared Lee

Simon & Schuster Books for Young Readers

New York London Toronto Sydney

You're having a nightmare, the monsters draw near.
You try to wake up, but you can't. Now they're here!

You feel your heart pound as you race up a tree.
The monsters surround you, there's nowhere to flee.
This dream is too scary, you must make it stop.

You cross all your fingers and call out . . .

"DREAM HOP!"

You're in a new place, a grand castle, it seems.

You say to yourself, "Good riddance, bad dreams!"

But out from the shadows there rides a bold knight,
who pulls out a sword and prepares for a fight.
"Let's duel!" he cries. "Get thee hither, chop-chop!"

You back away slowly and holler . . .

"DREAM HOP!"

But next thing you know something's wrapped round your knee.
A something that's dragging you under the sea.
Eight tentacles grab you from bottom to top.

You gasp one more breath and you gurgle . . .

"DREAM HOP!"

You're safe on a ship, no more swimming for you.

You say to yourself, "Surely THIS dream will do!"

When out comes a pirate, his evil eyes flashing.
"A stowaway, men! We must give him a lashing!"
You start to feel seasick—it's time for a swap.

You say to yourself, "No more nightmares for me!"

For Kyle, the original Dream Hopper, with love—J. D.

To my wife P. J., who made my dreams come true—J. L.

SIMON & SCHUSTER BOOKS FOR YOUNG READERS · An imprint of Simon & Schuster Children's Publishing Division · 1230 Avenue of the Americas, New York, New York 10020 · Text copyright © 2005 by Julia Durango · Illustrations copyright © 2005 by Jared Lee · All rights reserved, including the right of reproduction in whole or in part in any form. · SIMON & SCHUSTER BOOKS FOR YOUNG READERS is a trademark of Simon & Schuster, Inc. · Book design by Lucy Ruth Cummins · The text for this book is set in Aunt Mildred. · The illustrations for this book are rendered in ink and dyes. · Manufactured in China · 10 9 8 7 6 5 4 3 2 1 · CIP data for this book is available from the Library of Congress. ISBN 0-689-87163-5 (ISBN-13: 978-0-689-87163-4)